William and the School Report
by Richmal Crompton

It was the last day of term. The school had
broken up, and William was making his slow
way home. He walked draggingly, his eyes fixed
on the ground. But it was not the thought of the
four weeks of holiday that was worrying
William. It was a suspicion, that he wasn't going
to have the four weeks of holiday.

The whole trouble had begun with William's
headmaster. William's father had happened to
meet him in the train going up to town, and
had asked him how William was getting on.
The headmaster had replied that his writing
was atrocious and he didn't seem able to spell
the simplest word or do the simplest sum.
Then, brightening, he suggested that William
should have coaching during the holidays.

atrocious: shocking

Mr Parkinson, one of the Junior form masters who lived near the school, would be at home for the four weeks, and had offered to coach backward boys. An hour a day. It would do William, said the headmaster, all the good in the world. Give him an entirely new start. Nothing like coaching. Nothing at all. William's father was impressed. He thanked the headmaster, and said that he would let him know definitely later on.

William was at first speechless with horror. When he found speech it was an appeal to justice.

"In the *holidays*," he exclaimed wildly. "There's *lors* against it. I'm sure there's *lors* against it. I've never heard of *anyone* having lessons in the holidays. Not *anyone!* I bet even *slaves* didn't have lessons in the holidays. I bet if they knew about it in Parliament, there'd be an inquest about it. Besides I shall only get ill with overworkin' an' get brain fever same as they do in books, an' then you'll have to pay doctors' bills an' p'raps," he said darkly, "you'll have to pay for my funeral too. I don't see how *anyone* could go on workin' like that for months an' *months* without ever stoppin' once an' not get brain fever and die of it. Anyone'd think you *wanted* me to die. An' if I did die I shun't be surprised if the judge did something to you about it."

His father replied, coolly, "I'm quite willing to risk it."

"An' I don't like Mr Parkinson," went on William gloomily, "he's always cross."

"Perhaps I can arrange it with one of the others," said Mr Brown.

"I don't like any of them," said William, still more gloomily. "They're all always cross."

Then he burst out again: "It's not fair havin' lessons in the holidays."

"It's because your work at school fails to reach a high standard," said Mr Brown.

"How d'you know?" said William after a moment's thought. "How d'you know it does? You've not seen my report. We don't get 'em till the last day."

"Your headmaster told me."

"Ole Markie?" said William. "Well I like that. I *like* that. He doesn't teach me at all. He doesn't teach me anythin' at all. I bet he was jus' makin' it up for somethin' to say to you. He'd got to say somethin' an' he couldn't think of anythin' else to say. I bet he tells everyone he meets that their son isn't doing well at school jus' for somethin' to say."

"All right," said William's father firmly, "I'll make no arrangements till I have seen your report. If it's a better one than it usually is, of course, you needn't have coaching."

William felt relieved. There were four weeks before the end of the term. Anything might happen. His father might forget about it altogether. Mr Parkinson might develop some disease. It was even possible that his report might be better. He watched Mr Parkinson narrowly for any signs of illness. He even made an effort to display intelligence and interest in class.

And now the last day of the term had come, and the prospect of holiday coaching loomed ahead. His father had not forgotten. Only last night he had reminded William that it depended on his report whether or not he was to have

lessons in the holidays. Mr Parkinson looked
almost revoltingly healthy, and in his pocket
William carried the worst report he had ever
had. He had read it in the cloakroom and it had
justified his fears. He had wild notions of
altering it. The word 'poor' could, he thought,
easily be changed to 'good', but remarks such as
'Seems to take no interest at all in this subject'
would read rather oddly after the comment
'good'.

William
walked slowly
and draggingly.
His father
would demand
the report, and
at once make

arrangements for the holiday coaching.

There didn't seem to be any escape. If he
destroyed the report and pretended that he had
lost it, his father would only write to the school
for another, and they'd probably make the next
one even more damning to pay him out for
giving them extra trouble. To make things worse

an aunt of his father's (whom William had not seen for several years) was coming over for the day. Having reached the road in which his home was, he halted. His father was probably coming home for lunch because of the aunt. He might be at home now. The moment when the report should be demanded was a moment to be postponed as far as possible. He needn't go home just yet. He turned aside into a wood, and wandered on aimlessly.

"If ever I get into Parliament," he muttered, "I'll pass a *lor* against reports."

He turned a bend in the path and came face to face with an old lady. William felt outraged by the sight of her – old ladies had no right to be in woods.

"I'm afraid I've lost my way, little boy," she said breathlessly. "I was directed to take a short cut from the station to the village through the wood, and I think I must have made a mistake."

William looked at her in disgust. She was nearly half a mile from the path that was a short cut from the station to the village.

"What part of the village d'you want to get to?" he said.

"Mr Brown's house," said the old lady, "I'm expected there for lunch."

The horrible truth struck William. This was his father's aunt, who was coming over for the day. He saw that she was peering at him with an expression of delight.

"But it's William," she said. "I remember you quite well. I'm your Aunt Augusta. What a good thing I happened to meet you, dear! You can take me home with you."

William was disconcerted for a moment. They were in reality only a very short distance from his home. But it was no part of William's plan to return home at once.

He considered the matter in silence for a minute, then said: "All right. You c'n come along with me."

"Thank you, my dear boy," said the old lady brightening. "Thank you. That will be very nice.

I shall quite enjoy having a little talk with you."

William led her further and further into the heart of the wood and away from his home. She told him stories of her far off childhood.

As they went on into the wood, however, she grew silent and rather breathless.

"Are we – nearly there, dear boy?" she said.

They had almost reached the end of the wood, and another few minutes would have brought them out into the main road, where a bus would take them to William's home. William still had no intention of going home.

He sat down on a fallen tree and said: "I'm afraid we're lost. We must've took the wrong turning. This wood goes on for miles an' miles. People've sometimes been lost for days."

"With – with no food?"

"Yes, with no food."

"B-but, they must have died surely?"

"Yes," said William,

"quite a lot of 'em were dead when they found 'em."

Aunt Augusta gave a little gasp of terror. William's heart was less stony than he liked to think. Her terror touched him and he relented.

"Look here," he said, "I think p'raps that path'll get us out. Let's try that path."

"No," she panted. "I can't walk another step just now."

"Well, I'll go," said William. "I'll go an' see if it leads to the road."

"No, you *certainly* mustn't," said Aunt Augusta sharply. "We must at all costs keep together. You'll miss your way and we shall both be lost separately. I've read of that happening in books. People lost in forests and one going on to find the way and losing the others. No, I'm certainly not going to risk that. I *forbid* you going a yard without me, William, and I'm much too exhausted to walk any more just at present."

William, who had by now tired of the adventure said: "Well … s'pose I leave some sort of trail same as they do in books."

"But what can you leave a trail of?" said Aunt Augusta.

Suddenly William's face shone as if illuminated by a light within. "I've got an envelope in my pocket," he said. "I'll tear that up, I mean –" he added, "it's a case of life and death, isn't it?"

"Do be careful then, dear boy," said Aunt Augusta. "Drop it every *inch* of the way. I hope it's something you can spare, by the way?"

"Oh yes," William assured her, "it's something I can spare all right."

He took the report out of his pocket, and began to tear it into tiny fragments.

The Day I Took the Rabbit Home
by Kaye Umansky

"Right," said Miss Archer. "Who's taking the rabbit home this weekend?"

We all looked around at each other. Nobody's hand was up.

"Come on," said Miss Archer. "Whose turn is it?"

It was nearly home time on Friday. Nobody cared whose turn it was.

"Check the chart, please, Chrissy," said Miss Archer.

Chrissy went over and checked it.

"It says Felicity, Miss," said Chrissy.

"Oh dear," sighed Miss Archer. "She's absent. Vineeta, could you take Bertie this weekend?"

"Sorry, Miss. We're going to my gran's," said Vineeta.

"Gemma? What about you?"

"Mum says I can't any more, Miss," said
Gemma.

"Well," said Miss Archer. "I suppose I could
ask Mr Nash if he'd put him in his shed.
Unless there's anybody else who …
Ah."

She relaxed. A lone hand was
waving in the air.

It was mine.

I don't know why I offered. I'd never taken
much notice of Bertie before. He's just the class
rabbit. He's brown and a bit mad. I leave it to
others – the girls, mainly – to clean his hutch
and bring in carrots. He doesn't seem much of a
pet to me. He doesn't do anything except eat
and kick his bedding around.

But he deserves better than a weekend in old
Gnasher's shed. Gnasher's what we call Mr
Nash, our school caretaker. He's really
grumpy and has two huge dogs
called Duke and Hunter.
Somehow, I don't think any
of them are rabbit lovers.

"Well done, Pete," beamed Miss Archer.

"I'm sure he won't be any trouble. Your mum won't mind?"

"Oh no," I said. Though I suspected she might, a bit. "No problem."

"How will you get the hutch home?"

"I'll get someone to help." Well, I only live five minutes away.

"Good. Don't forget the Rabbit Book."

The Rabbit Book contains information about Bertie's likes and dislikes, tips about cleaning his hutch and how to pick him up (not by his ears), and the vet's number. Stuff like that.

The bell rang. Everybody made for the door, except me. I'd lumbered myself with Bertie.

"I'll help you, Pete," offered Chrissy. She lives down my street. It made sense.

"Okay," I said, stuffing the Rabbit Book in my pocket. "Thanks."

We took an end each. It was heavier than I thought. Bertie scrabbled about inside. His dish slid down to my end, scattering dried food on my trainers. Chrissy nearly dropped her end. The water bottle fell off and rolled under a radiator.

"Are you all right with that?" asked Miss
Archer.

"Yes, Miss," we said. We staggered up the
classroom, knocking over chairs and pots of
felt-tips. Miss Archer followed, tutting and
picking things up.

"I'll leave you to it, then," said Miss Archer,
and hurried into the staff room.

It was windy outside. We lurched across the
playground. Bertie was going bonkers, racing up
and down.

Some of the infants were hanging around, waiting to be picked up. We knocked one over by accident and she cried a bit.

"Sorry," we said.

We got to the pavement.

"I've got to put it down," said Chrissy, and did. Bertie slid down the slope, along with his dish. I dropped my end with a thump. The water bottle fell into the road, where it was run over by a lorry. Great.

"I think I've got a splinter," said Chrissy. The hutch lay across the pavement. We were getting nasty looks from passers-by.

"Ready for the next bit?" I asked.

"I suppose so."

We bent down, got a grip and lifted.

Slowly, we shuffled along to the crossing.

Vince, the lollipop man, said, "What you got in

there, then? An elephant?" And laughed loudly
at his own feeble joke.

Crossing the road was really embarrassing.
The Rabbit Book fell out of my pocket. All
the pages came loose and blew away in the
wind. We had to put the hutch down and go
running after them.

Did I say I lived close to the school? It
didn't feel like it that day. By the time we
got to my house, both of us
felt like we'd climbed
Mount Everest.

It's only a small house and there are a lot of
us to fit in. Me, Mum, Dad, Gran, my little
sister Molly, baby George and Pushkin, our cat.

We're known as the Greenaways. When Chrissy
and I arrived, there was nobody in apart from
Molly and Gran, who was snoozing on the sofa.
Dad was out with George. Mum was still at
work. No sign of Pushkin.

"What you got there, Pete?" asked Molly,
when she opened the door. "Ooh. A bunny."

"School rabbit," I wheezed. "Got him for the
weekend."

"Ooh, good, hooway! Can he sleep in my
bed?"

"No, he's staying in his hutch. In my room.
Come on, Chrissy. Last bit."

Some paint got chipped off the door frame.
Straw, food and a load of yucky little black
pellets fell all over the hall carpet. We tried not
to tread them in, but it was hard not to.

We puffed our way up the stairs, scraping the
wallpaper. We tried to turn into my bedroom.
The hutch got stuck in the doorway and Chrissy
got her finger jammed and she knocked over my
lamp. I've got the smallest bedroom. It's full of
stuff. But it does have a tiny balcony. I keep my
bike out there, along with a couple of dead

plants. It's one of Pushkin's favourite places. She
likes to sit out there and watch the birds.

Finally, we got the hutch in and dumped it on
the floor, beside the broken lamp. Then I took
Chrissy down to the kitchen to get
a plaster for her finger, which
was bleeding. Some blood
dripped on the stairs going
down.

Honestly. I'd only been
home five minutes and the
house looked like a cross
between a farmyard and
an abattoir.

I offered Chrissy a
glass of lemonade, but
she said her friend
was coming round.
She'd had enough
and I can't say I
blamed her.

When she went, I
tried getting the blood off the stair carpet with a
damp flannel but I only spread it around more.

When I reached the landing, I thought I'd better check on Bertie.

All was quiet, anyway. That, I discovered, was because he wasn't there!

His hutch was empty.

"Molly!" I yelled. "What have you done with the rabbit?"

Silence.

I went into her room. She was sitting on her bed, all innocent, playing with her dolls.

"Where's Bertie?"

"I twied to cuddle him," said Molly. "But he didn't want to."

"So where is he?"

"Out on your balcony. Having a walk."

"Whaaaaat?" I couldn't believe my ears.

I raced back to my room and tripped over the fallen lamp, scraping my shin. Moaning, I hobbled to the door and threw it open.

Did I mention that the balcony's got steps leading down to the back garden? Well, it has. Down below, a chilling sight met my eyes. Bertie was racing round in circles, hotly pursued by Pushkin.

"Pushkin!" I yelled. "Stop that!"

I raced down the steps. Molly had left a stuffed kangaroo halfway down. It must have been out there for weeks, because it was soaking wet and really slippery. I stepped on it, my foot went out from under me and I slithered down to the bottom.

I was just in time to see Bertie bolt through a gap in the fence. Next door are the Parsons. They're not very friendly. Pushkin didn't follow. She crouched next to the hole, tail twitching. This was for two reasons:

1. It was a bit of a squeeze.
2. The Parsons own a huge dog called Butch.

"Bad cat! Get away!" I shouted.

She knew I was mad. I hurried over to the hole, pushed her to one side and peered through.

All I could see was the bottoms of dustbins. And the edge of Butch's kennel,

from which came a low growl.

Oh, heck.

The Parsons weren't in. I rang the doorbell for ages.

"What you gonna do, Pete?" asked Molly.

"I don't know. Get the stepladder, I suppose."

The stepladder lives down in the cellar, surrounded by a million tins of half-finished paint. I knocked one of the tins over and the top came off. Blue paint glugged all over the cellar floor. No time to deal with that, though.

I wrestled the ladder up the stairs and through the kitchen.

"You're getting the floor all painty," said Molly, helpfully.

"I'll clear it up later," I snapped. Butch's barking had reached a frenzy now.

I ran across the garden and set the stepladder in the flower bed, as close as I could to the fence.

"You're squashing Mummy's flowers," said Molly.

I ignored her and began to climb. The earth was soft and the ladder was really unsteady.

"Careful, Pete," said Molly.

"Look, I know what I'm doing, all right?" I said. "It's quite secure ..."

That was when I felt it slip to one side!

"It's falling," Molly warned me.

It was, too. Slowly, it keeled over into the fence, which collapsed, taking me with it.

As I lay face down, I felt something hot and slobbery lick my neck. Slowly, I raised my head and found myself staring into a pair of surprised, doggy eyes.

Butch, of course. He seemed in no rush to bite me. Maybe he'd eaten already!

At any rate there was no sign of
Bertie.

* * * * *

Some time later, I
sat in the kitchen while
my family
screamed
at me. Dad had come home first with George,
so he had the first go, with Gran chipping in.
Then Mum arrived and it started all over again.
Stuff about new carpets and straw and
droppings and chipped paint and broken lamps
and blood stains and blue footprints and
trampled flowers and collapsed fences.

I just sat and worried. Where was Bertie? All
right, so I'm not exactly keen on him, but he
was my responsibility.

Butch couldn't really have eaten him, could
he? Surely there would have been some
gruesome evidence. An ear or something.
Wouldn't there?

What concerned me most was what Miss
Archer would say on Monday. I felt so queasy

thinking about it, I could hardly eat my tea.

When I'd forced down the last fish finger, I volunteered to help clean the house, but my kind offer was turned down. I can't say I was sorry. I was covered in bruises. Not that anyone seemed to care.

Molly and I did a tour of both gardens before dark, but Bertie was still nowhere to be found. I wandered in and asked Mum if I could change schools, but she said no and went on rubbing the carpet with white spirit. Dad was trying to fix the broken lamp and just glared. No joy there.

So I went up to my room and sat sadly looking at the empty rabbit hutch. It had a haunted air.

That night, I had bad dreams.

* * * * *

The following morning, I was awoken by a loud wail, followed by running footsteps.

I rushed down in my pyjamas. Now what?

My entire family was in the living room. Mum was jiggling George. Dad had his arm around Gran, who was pale and gibbering and holding one of her fluffy slippers upside down. They were both staring down at a neat little pile of brown rabbit droppings! Gran usually leaves her slippers parked by the sofa so she can slip her bare feet in when she sits down with her morning cuppa. This morning, she had got more than she had bargained for.

Molly sat on the sofa, cuddling and cooing over the culprit.

Bertie, of course.

He looked just the same. Mad as a hatter – but all in one piece. He had come in through the kitchen cat flap and helped himself from the vegetable basket during the night.

Talk about relief!

I won't bore you with the rest of the weekend. About how he blew up with all the carrots he'd eaten and we had to take him to the vet, and how much it cost and what Dad

had to say about that.
And the trip to the
pet shop for a
replacement water
bottle and more
straw, which came
out of my pocket
money.

Anyway, there I
was, back in school
on Monday. Miss
Archer finished calling the register, then said:
"Where's Bertie, Pete?"

"Dad's bringing him at lunchtime," I said.

"Oh, that's kind. Did you enjoy having him
for the weekend?"

I caught Chrissy's eye. I'd told her all about it
on the way to school. She'd nearly killed herself
laughing. Can you believe it?

"It was – interesting," I said. Chrissy gave a
snort.

"Good. I hope you remembered to bring back
the Rabbit Book."

I reached into my pocket and took out a

handful of dirty, crumpled bits of paper.

"My word!" said Miss Archer. "It's in a bit of a state, isn't it?"

"Sorry," I mumbled. "Bit of an accident crossing the road."

"Well, perhaps you'd like to spend break time copying it out."

No. I wouldn't like to. But I had to, of course. To be fair, Chrissy stayed in and helped me.

Dad dropped Bertie off at lunchtime.

"Thanks, Mr Greenaway," said Miss Archer, gazing fondly into the hutch. "Dear little Bertie. I hope he wasn't any trouble."

Hmm.

Don't Mess with Mrs Mattock
by Jeremy Strong

Jodi had passed that door every day for the last four years, ever since she had started at Clophill School. Clophill was a perfectly normal school – or so Jodi thought, but that was before all the trouble began. The big trouble. And it came from behind that door.

It all came down to a dare, and Martin Blagdon started it. It was break time when Martin stopped outside that door and stared at it. There was a small, neat, metal label on the front.

"What's in there?" he asked. "I've always wondered. I know what's behind every door in this school, except this one." He banged on the door with his fist.

"*Rrrrrrrrrrrrr.*"

It was a low sound, like some distant machine. "It's someone breathing," Jodi whispered, her eyes big.

"Yeah," snorted Martin. "There's a big, buggy bogeyman in there!"

Martin laughed and pressed the side of his head against the door. "It's not breathing," he said. "It's a machine; probably something to do with the central heating."

Now four of them had their heads pressed against the door, listening.

"*Rrrrrrrrrr.*"

"Just what do you think you are doing?" It was the head, Miss Snodgrass. "Get away from that door at once and go outside! Don't let me ever see you back there again!"

The children scuttled out to the playground, where they stood in a corner, looking at each other.

"Blimey!" breathed Sanjeev. "She was a bit angry!"

Jodi slowly shook her head. "Snodgrass wasn't being angry, Sanjeev. She was panicking."

"Panicking?" said the others.

"Yes. She wanted us away from that door as quickly as possible. Didn't you notice?"

"You're right." said Martin. "Snodgrass didn't want us anywhere near that door. Why not?"

Sheree narrowed her eyes. "There's something in there that she doesn't want us to know about."

"Yeah! A mountain of crisp packets! A billion cans of cola!"

"That's crazy," Sanjeev said. "Snodgrass wouldn't keep stuff in there for us."

"What about the breathing we heard?" asked Jodi.

"It was a machine," insisted Martin.

"Breathing," Sheree and Jodi said together.

"Okay, I bet you it's a machine in there. In fact, I dare you to find out," said Martin.

"All right, you're on," said Jodi.

"How are we going to get in there?" asked Sanjeev.

"Get the keys from the office," Martin said.

"Blimey," muttered Sanjeev.

"Don't keep saying 'blimey' like that," complained Sheree.

"Why not?"

"It's rude."

"Who says?"

"My mum."

"Blimey!" murmured Sanjeev in surprise.

Sheree kicked him. At that moment the whistle went and everyone went back in to school.

Jodi was very quiet in class. She was thinking

about the keys in the office and her head was slowly filling with a sneaky plan. All at once her hand shot up in the air.

"Jodi?" asked Mr Reece.

"I'm bursting! Got to go!" Jodi rushed off. She made straight for the school office, where the secretary was typing. Jodi poked her head round the corner of the door. The keys were hanging on a board behind the secretary's head.

"Please Miss, some boy has been sick down by the library."

"Oh dear." The secretary grabbed a towel

and a bowl and hurried off to the library. Jodi snaffled the keys and whizzed back to class. She couldn't wait to tell the others.

When afternoon break came Jodi showed the keys to her friends.

"Wow!" Martin breathed. "I never thought you'd ... I mean, wow!"

"Blimey!" whispered Sanjeev and Sheree kicked him again.

"You know what this means?" asked Martin. "We have the keys and that means we have to go and open that door."

The others nodded. Jodi had been thinking about this next bit, too. "Sheree watches one end of the corridor. Sanjeev watches the other. The rest of us open the door."

They had to wait five minutes or so before the coast was clear. Jodi had her ear to the door.

"*Rrrrrrrrrrr.*"

"Breathing," she muttered.

"Machine," said Martin.

At last they got a 'thumbs up' from the lookouts. There were about fifteen keys on the big ring. Jodi wondered how long it would take to find the right one. It took seven tries. Jodi glanced at Martin. He nodded and she pulled the door open.

The cupboard was big and in complete darkness. It seemed to go back a long way and

it was full of bits and pieces of old
school equipment. Much to
their surprise there was also
a dinner plate on the floor
near the door. There was no
food on it, but it wasn't
clean either. There had been
food on it, but something,
or someone, had eaten it.

"Come on, let's go back,"
Jodi whispered.

"Scaredy-cat," Martin said.

Then they heard the growl.
"Rrrrrrrrrrrrrrrrrr." It was
much louder this time and coming from the very
depths of the cupboard. It was definitely not a
machine. Even Martin turned white.

"I think we'd better get out and ..." he
began, but a deep snarl drowned his last few
words.

"Too late, little boy. Much too late!" There
was a clattering and clawing from the back of
the cupboard, and as the children started to
back out, a giant monster burst upon them.

She was huge. She was horrible. Most of her bottom half was like a fat old lady, with two fat legs in thick socks wobbling about on spindly, red shoes. There were wide hips and an enormous backside hidden under a thick, check skirt. Then came the truly gruesome bit. The top half of this creature was like a giant stag beetle, bursting out of a horrible woollen cardigan, and with a head full of snapping jaws.

"Aaargh!" screamed Jodi and Martin, while Sheree slid to the ground in a dead faint.

"Aha! Dinner!" screeched the monster. She

snatched up Sheree and burst out into the
corridor.

Staff came running from every direction. Miss
Snodgrass was demanding to know what was
happening, but as soon as she saw the
monster she knew for herself.

"Who let Mrs Mattock out of the
cupboard? How did this happen?" she
demanded. "That cupboard is strictly out of
bounds. That is why it says 'PRIVATE' on the
front." The head teacher caught sight of Jodi.
"Jodi? Was this your doing?"

Jodi could only gulp and nod. Miss
Snodgrass drew herself up. "I shall deal with
you later. Meanwhile we have an emergency
on our hands. Mrs Mattock hasn't been fed
today. She'll be looking for food."

"She's already got some," Martin burst out.
"She ran off with Sheree."

"Oh no, oh no! What a tragedy!" Miss
Snodgrass shook her head. "What shall I tell her
parents?"

"We could try and get her back," suggested
Jodi.

"I absolutely forbid it. Mrs Mattock is very dangerous."

"But how did she get like that?" asked Sanjeev. "She's horrible! She's half human, half beetle!"

By this time Mr Reece had also reached the scene. They stood in the corridor, staring out through the window at the playground, where Mrs Mattock was racing round and round, clicking her jaws, roaring and snarling and still carrying poor Sheree. Every so often Sheree would wake from her faint, scream and faint again.

"Poor Mrs Mattock," Mr Reece murmured.

"She used to be such a good teacher, brilliant at teaching maths. But gradually, day by day, she got more and more cross – not with children, just cross with everything."

"Everything," repeated Miss Snodgrass. "The staff, school dinners, coffee money, the crossing patrol, inspections, tests – everything."

Mr Reece nodded. "She always used to make a big thing of teaching children multiplication tables. And then when children were allowed to use calculators instead, she just flipped. She changed overnight. I was the last to see her normal. I think she stayed here overnight and when I got back in the morning she was, she was ..."

Mr Reece almost broke down as he pointed

to the monster outside. "She had changed – into that poor, crazy creature out there."

Jodi was horrified. What a terrible tale! And now Mrs Mattock had Sheree, and it was all Jodi's fault. It was up to her to do something about it. While the others stood at the window talking, Jodi slipped away. Nobody noticed for several minutes until Martin suddenly gave a yell.

"It's Jodi! She's gone out there!"

They watched as Jodi approached the snorting beast. Mrs Mattock swung round, still clutching Sheree.

"We should help her," said Sanjeev, but Miss Snodgrass told them to stay put.

Outside Mrs Mattock glared at Jodi and began to stamp the ground with her fat, red shoes, like some wild and savage beast about to charge. Her antennae whisked one way then another, and her tiny, beady eyes glowed red as she fixed them on the small figure of the girl.

Sheree fainted again.

"It's only me," Jodi said softly. "I'm Jodi. I'm your friend, Mrs Mattock. I know all about you. It's all right. I won't hurt you."

The monster hissed, her enormous backside swaying this way and that. "You hurt me? Don't be stupid!" she hissed. "I am Mrs Mattock, The Giant Beetlewoman. I could crunch you up like a boiled sweet. I could squash you beneath my feet like a piece of chewing gum. What do you say to that?"

Jodi swallowed hard and cleared her throat with a little cough. "I say, tell me what six threes are, please."

"Eighteen!" roared The Giant Beetlewoman.

Jodi clapped her hands and smiled. "You're so clever! What about eight sevens?"

"Eight sevens? No, no! You're trying to trick me! I always forget what eight sevens are!"

"Don't you know the answer, Mrs Mattock? Surely you know the answer to eight sevens? It's so easy."

Giant Beetlewoman twisted her head this way and that as she struggled to think of the correct number. "I need to use my fingers," she cried. "But look, they are claws now! I cannot count any longer!"

"Why don't you use your toes?" suggested Jodi cheerfully. "You still have toes.

I'm sure you can do it, Mrs Mattock. You have always been such a wizard at maths."

Giant Beetlewoman stared down at her feet. "Eight sevens," she said over and over. "I should be able to work that out easily. The girl is right. I could use my toes."

Mrs Mattock sat down, with her legs stretched out in front of her. She put down Sheree, who was beginning to stir from her fainting fit. Giant Beetlewoman took off her shoes and pulled off her thick socks. She wiggled her toes and smiled.

At least, Jodi thought she smiled. It was difficult to tell when you were staring at a giant beetle head. Mrs Mattock gave her toes another wiggle and then set to counting. "Eight sevens. Let's see, one, two, three, four …"

Behind Mrs Mattock, Martin and Sanjeev were creeping toward Sheree, who had just fainted for the ninth time. They grabbed an arm each and began dragging Sheree away.

"… Eight, nine, ten, run out of toes so start again. One, two, three, four …"

Jodi waited until she was quite sure that

Sheree was safely back at school. "Mrs Mattock, can I help you? What are seven sevens?"

"Oh, that's a doddle, my child," said the monster, in an almost normal voice, and Jodi was surprised to notice that the beetle body somehow looked ... well, less like a beetle. "The answer is forty-nine."

"So eight sevens will only be seven more than that," Jodi explained.

"Of course! Of course! Why didn't I think of that? I don't know. Sometimes my brain is no better than a beetle's. So, the answer is ... fifty-six!"

"Well done, Mrs Mattock!" cried Jodi. "You did it!"

Giant Beetlewoman grinned back at Jodi. "I did do it, didn't I? And look – my claws are turning into fingers. Oh my, what a funny day I'm having."

It was true. Giant Beetlewoman was turning back into the old Mrs Mattock. She still had fat legs and a giant backside, but at least she was human. They marched back into school, hand in hand, to a great chorus of cheers and a single "blimey!" from Sanjeev.

And that is almost the end of the story. Mrs Mattock was back to normal. In fact, Jodi became quite fond of Mrs Mattock and went to see her once a week for extra lessons. In due course she grew up to become the greatest mathematician in the world. You see, Mrs Mattock really had been a terrific maths teacher all along.

Mrs Mattock even went back to teaching maths at Clophill School. But the children always knew when she was getting cross. Not only did she start frowning, but sometimes it looked as if her forehead began to sprout little, beetle-like antennae. She would wave her long, thin arms and clack her fingers like the jaws of some giant insect. Then the class remembered: don't mess with Mrs Mattock!